The LAST FIREHAWK

The Cloud Kingdom

by
Katrina Charman

SCHOLASTIC INC.

The LAST FIREHAWK

Read All the Books

1 The Ember Stone

2 The Crystal Caverns

3 The Whispering Oak

4 Lullaby Lake

5 The Shadowlands

6 The Battle for Perodia

7 The Cloud Kingdom

8 The Silver Swamp

More books coming soon!

scholastic.com/lastfirehawk

Table of Contents

For Maddie, Piper and Riley. —KC

Text copyright © 2019 by Katrina Charman

Illustrations copyright © 2019 by Scholastic Inc.

Library of Congress Cataloging-in-Publication Data

Names: Charman, Katrina, author. | Charman, Katrina. Last firehawk ; 7. Title: The Cloud Kingdom / by Katrina Charman. Description: First edition. | New York, NY : Branches/Scholastic Inc., 2019. | Series: The last firehawk ; 7 | Summary: Now that Thorn has been defeated, Tag and his friend Skyla embark on a new quest, to find Blaze's lost family and the other firehawks who disappeared through a portal to the Cloud Kingdom; but the Cloud Kingdom is full of new dangers, and when giant birds seize Blaze and carry her off Tag and Skyla are left to try and free their friend--with only a magic map to guide them, and the threat of the shadowy shape that seems to be following them.

Identifiers: LCCN 2018060391| ISBN 9781338307177 (pbk. : alk. paper) | ISBN 9781338307184 (hardcover : alk. paper) Subjects: LCSH: Owls—Juvenile fiction. | Squirrels—Juvenile fiction. | Animals, Mythical—Juvenile fiction. | Magic—Juvenile fiction. | Quests (Expeditions)—Juvenile fiction. | Adventure stories. | CYAC: Owls—Fiction. | Squirrels—Fiction. | Animals, Mythical—Fiction. | Magic—Fiction. | Adventure and adventurers—Fiction. | Fantasy. | LCGFT: Action and adventure fiction. Classification: LCC PZ7.1.C495 Cl 2019 | DDC [Fic]—dc23 LC record available at https://lccn.loc.gov/2018060391

10 9 8 7 6 5 4 3 2 1   19 20 21 22 23

Printed in China   62

First edition, December 2019

Illustrated by Judit Tondora

Edited by Katie Carella and Rachel Matson

Book design by Maria Mercado

~ INTRODUCTION ~

In the enchanted land of Perodia,
lies Valor Wood—a forest filled with magic and light. There, a wise owl named Grey leads the Owls of Valor. These brave warriors protect the creatures of the wood.

Tag, a small barn owl, and his friends Skyla and the last firehawk, Blaze, have finally defeated the evil vulture Thorn. But now they have a new challenge—to find Blaze's family and the rest of the lost firehawks. Their only clues are three golden firehawk feathers.

Tag, Skyla, and Blaze must all work together to find the hidden land known as the Cloud Kingdom.

Will these three friends discover what *really* happened to Blaze's family all those years ago?

The adventure continues . . .

PERODIA AND THE

Shifting Sands

Whispering Oak

Mossy Hills

Howling Caves

Valor Wood

Rocky Beach

N
W · E
S

CLOUD KINGDOM

Crystal Caverns

Jagged Mountains

Bubbling Bog

Lullaby Lake

The Shadowlands

Blue Bay

Fire Island

CHAPTER 1

A NEW JOURNEY

Valor Wood was filled with warm sunlight. The trees were thick and green, and the river sparkled blue. Perodia was full of life and magic now that Thorn had been defeated.

Tag and his friends Skyla and Blaze stood in the center of the wood. Grey, the leader of the Owls of Valor, stood beside them.

"The feathers showed Blaze that her family went to a kingdom in the clouds," Tag told Grey. "We should leave at once to find it."

Blaze held three golden feathers. Skyla had found the first one on Fire Island, and she found another in a cave in Valor Wood. The last feather had come from Thorn.

Grey looked at Blaze. "Are you sure you want to go on this new quest?" he asked her. "What if your family is no longer alive?"

Blaze nodded as she handed the feathers to Skyla. Skyla tucked them inside her armor for safekeeping. "Thorn said there are more firehawks," Blaze said. "I have to hope my family is among them."

"Thorn has lied to you before," Tag warned.

"Tell us what the magic feathers showed you again," she asked Blaze.

"Maybe there was a clue about where to start searching," said Tag.

Blaze closed her eyes, trying to remember.

"I saw firehawks on Fire Island," Blaze said. "One of them—their leader—plucked three golden feathers from her tail. Then there was a bright light and a door appeared out of nowhere." Blaze opened her eyes and looked at her friends. "Then the firehawks all disappeared through the door."

"A portal," Grey whispered, stroking his chin feathers. "A magical doorway that can only be opened by a magical object."

"Maybe the feathers are the key to opening the portal," Skyla said.

Blaze hopped up and down excitedly.

Grey looked unsure. "Perhaps," he said. "But you should take the Ember Stone with you, too. When it regains its powers, it could be useful."

Tag pulled the Ember Stone from his sack. It was dull and cold. Its magic used to glow, but the stone had not glowed since it sucked up Thorn's dark shadow. He placed it back into his sack.

The friends gathered their supplies and filled Tag's sack with fruit, nuts, and water. Tag took his dagger, and Skyla took her slingshot.

"Good luck," Grey said. "And stay on your guard. There are dangers beyond this land."

Tag took a last glance at Valor Wood—the beautiful trees and the tinkling stream. His home.

The three friends waved goodbye to Grey.

"To Fire Island!" Tag said. "We must find the portal to the Cloud Kingdom!"

And so their journey began.

RETURN TO
FIRE ISLAND

Tag and Blaze flew over the trees of Valor Wood. Skyla was on Blaze's back. Below they could see Blue Bay, and across the choppy waves was Fire Island.

They flew and flew, then landed on the beach at last.

Tag looked around and gasped. "Fire Island is so different!" he said. The last time they had visited, the trees were dying and there was no food to eat. But now . . .

"Look at the trees!" Skyla cried. They were covered with plump fruit hanging from every branch.

"And the flowers!" Blaze said.

Tag breathed in the wonderful smell. "It's amazing!" he said. "Everything Thorn and The Shadow destroyed has come back to life!"

The friends sat in a grassy clearing. Tag listened as the breeze gently rustled the leaves. He ate some berries, then paused.

His feathers tingled. He stood up.

"What's wrong?" Skyla asked.

"I think someone is watching us," Tag said.

Skyla pulled out her slingshot.

There was a sudden blur as something swung through the trees above them.

"There!" Tag yelled.

The friends chased after the creatures.

Skyla shouted, "Stop right there!"

Two small spider monkeys stood in the clearing. They had brown fur, long bushy tails, and white faces.

Tag remembered these monkeys from his first visit to the island. They had stolen berries from him.

Tag glared at them. "You again! Were you trying to steal our food?" he asked.

The monkeys shook their heads. "No," said one of the monkeys. "We have plenty of our own food. We're sorry about stealing from you before."

"We were only watching you," said the other monkey.

"Why?" Tag asked. He still felt uneasy.

The spider monkeys looked at the ground. "We were just curious. We don't get many visitors on Fire Island," the monkey continued.

The monkeys smiled and stepped forward. "I'm Mika, and this is Molly."

Blaze nudged Tag, and said, "Maybe they know something about the portal!"

"What's a portal?" Molly asked.

"A portal is a magical door," Blaze explained.

"Have you seen one here on the island?" Skyla asked.

The monkeys thought for a while. "What does a portal look like?" Mika asked.

"It looks like a magic doorway with bright light spilling out of it," Blaze replied. "We think the firehawks made it appear."

"We haven't seen anything like that. But maybe the portal is near the firehawk paintings," Molly suggested.

Tag, Skyla, and Blaze had discovered these paintings during their last trip to Fire Island.

"That's a good idea. Let's look there," Tag decided, packing away his sack.

"Thanks for your help!" said Blaze.

"Good luck!" called the monkeys as they scampered away.

The friends flew to the very top of Fire Island. The paintings were there on the rock, just as Tag remembered them. But there was no sign of the portal.

"Try holding the feathers near the paintings," Skyla suggested to Blaze.

Blaze held the three golden feathers in her beak, hoping for a magical sign. Nothing happened.

Blaze's head drooped. "I don't think the portal is here," she said.

Tag sighed. "How will we ever find the Cloud Kingdom?"

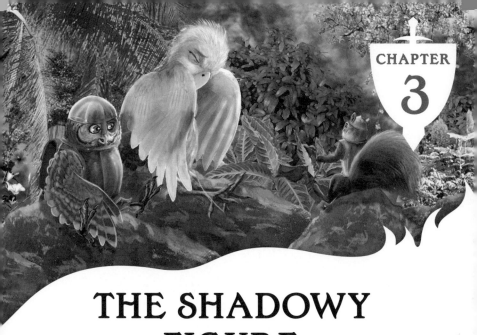

THE SHADOWY FIGURE

Blaze sat with her head in her wings.

Tag patted her shoulder and handed the feathers back to Skyla. "Do you remember *where* the portal was in your vision?" Tag asked.

Blaze shook her head. "I could only see the firehawks and the doorway, nothing more," she replied. "But those were both definitely on Fire Island."

Skyla's tail twitched. "We'll search the whole island then. It must be here somewhere."

Blaze jumped to her feet. "You're right! We just need to keep looking!"

Tag followed as they headed down the mountain. A creepy feeling crawled down his neck. He couldn't shake the sense that something was not right.

A dark figure moved in some tall trees nearby. Tag took a step toward it.

"Who's there?" he whispered.

The figure moved and ran deeper into the woods. Tag raced after it.

"Come back!" he called. The woods were dark, full of twisting trees. Tag slowed down. He couldn't see the shadowy figure anymore. He took a few more steps when—

SNAP! A twig broke behind him. He spun around with his dagger.

"Skyla!" Tag cried. "You scared me!"

"What are you doing?" Blaze asked.

"I saw something . . ." Tag began. "Never mind. Let's just keep looking for the portal."

Tag kept his dagger close just in case the strange figure appeared again.

The friends searched the island from the very top, all the way down to the bottom of the volcano.

"There's nothing here," Blaze said.

"Let's check the beach," Skyla suggested.

A large, wrinkled turtle sat at the edge of the water. It waved a flipper at them.

"Thaddeus!" Blaze called out, running to greet their friend.

"Hi! What are you three doing here?" Thaddeus asked. He spoke very s-l-o-w-l-y.

"We're searching for a portal," Tag said. "We think the firehawks went through it to get to the Cloud Kingdom. Have you seen one?"

"Hmmmmmm," Thaddeus said. "I haven't seen a portal. But I remember a place where the firehawks gathered. There is a circle of tall rocks deep in the forest."

"Maybe it's there!" Skyla said.

"Thank you, Thaddeus," Blaze said.

They said goodbye to Thaddeus and hurried off through the trees. The sky was darkening as night settled in.

After hours of searching for the circle of tall rocks, Tag dropped his sack to the ground. "Let's make camp and search again in the morning," he said.

They made a nest using branches and leaves. Then they quickly fell asleep.

Tag awoke suddenly. It was still night, but something sparkled in the darkness. It was coming from beneath Skyla's armor.

"Skyla! Blaze!" Tag shouted. "Wake up!"

Skyla and Blaze awoke.

"What's wrong?" Skyla asked sleepily.

Then she saw her sparkling armor. "The feathers are glowing again!" she cried.

THE PORTAL

Skyla pulled the three golden feathers out of her armor. The clearing sparkled with glittering light.

"Look!" Blaze shouted, pointing behind Tag. "The circle of tall rocks that Thaddeus told us about is right there!"

Tag gasped. "Blaze, your eyes!"

Blaze's eyes were sparkling gold, just like the feathers!

"What's happening to your sack?" Skyla asked, pointing at Tag's sack.

Pale sparkly light shone out of it.

Tag quickly opened his sack. The Ember Stone shone as bright as the moon.

"Be careful, Tag," Blaze warned. "It might be hot."

Tag gently touched the stone. "It's cold," he said.

"That's strange," Skyla said. She wrinkled her nose. "The Ember Stone usually burns hot and purple when it shines."

"Maybe it uses a different kind of magic to open the door," Tag suggested.

Blaze nodded and picked up the stone. "I think one of these tall rocks might be the portal," she said. She moved away from the circle of rocks. As she did, the light in her eyes flickered, and the light of the feathers and of the Ember Stone grew duller.

Skyla gasped. "I think you're right!"

"Move closer to the rocks," Tag said.

Blaze hopped closer, and everything grew brighter.

"See? The feathers are showing us the way!" she said.

She stood in the center of the rock circle and slowly turned to face each one. "If one of these rocks is the portal, then it should light up," she said.

When Blaze faced the final rock, the Ember Stone and the three feathers grew so bright that Tag and Skyla had to shield their eyes. The light made an outline of a doorway on the rock.

"The magic portal!" Tag said, jumping up and down.

A loud scraping sound filled the air as the tall rock began to tremble. It started to crumble away, turning to dust. And there, in the middle of the clearing was a sparkling staircase.

Tag gazed into the portal. The stairs seemed to wind up and up and up, as far as he could see. He thought about the dark figure again, and shivered.

"This is our chance to find the firehawks!" Blaze said. Then she hopped through the portal, taking the stairs two at a time.

Skyla scampered in after her.

Tag glanced around but saw no sign of the shadowy figure.

"Wait for me!" he called.

Tag hurried up the staircase. He climbed a few steps, then stopped and glanced back. He wanted to make sure no one followed them through the portal. But Fire Island had already disappeared. All Tag saw was a dark wall of stone.

Tag continued on. There was no going back now.

Blaze and Skyla waited for him to catch up, but Tag called out to them. "Keep going!"

A light at the top of the staircase grew brighter and brighter as they climbed. Finally, Tag could see a blazing sun in a blue sky, filled with fluffy white clouds.

"The Cloud Kingdom!" Blaze exclaimed.

INTO THE CLOUD KINGDOM

Blaze hopped up and down. Skyla cheered and joined her friend. Tag couldn't help but smile. Maybe they would find Blaze's family after all.

"I can't believe we did it!" Skyla said.

"Hooray!" Blaze shouted. "We found the Cloud Kingdom!" She stopped suddenly. "Now we need to find my family. Where should we look?"

Blaze and Skyla both turned to Tag.

Tag laughed. "Calm down," he said. "Let's try to figure out where we are first."

He looked around. The Cloud Kingdom was like nothing he had seen before. This world was filled with color. There were flowers and plants of blue and red and yellow and purple. The air smelled as sweet as sugar plums and candy.

Tag stepped forward, but the ground felt strange beneath his feet. It was soft, white, and fluffy. Tag was walking on clouds.

"Watch this!" Blaze shouted. She leaped in the air. When she landed, she bounced up, then down again.

"My turn!" Skyla said. She flipped in the air, then landed on another fluffy cloud. "Let's go explore!"

Tag moved slowly. He didn't like the feeling of bouncing up and down. It made his tummy feel funny. Instead, he flew after his friends.

First they explored a patch of strange trees. "Look at those!" Tag called.

The trees had bright yellow trunks that curved out of the ground like giant springs. On the end of their twisting branches were pastel-colored flowers. The flowers looked just like cotton-candy balls.

Then the friends wandered past huge rocks that looked like they were made from crystal. The sunshine shone through them, filling the air with tiny rainbows.

Everywhere they went, they found more strange and wonderful sights.

Tag landed beside his friends. He still had an uneasy feeling.

"What's wrong, Tag?" Skyla asked, bouncing over.

Blaze joined them.

"Where is everyone?" Tag asked. "We've been exploring the Cloud Kingdom for hours, but we haven't seen one creature. Not even an insect."

"Maybe they are asleep?" Skyla said.

"That's another thing," Tag replied. "When we walked through the portal, it was still night in Perodia. How is the sun already up here?"

Blaze shrugged.

"You worry too much, Tag," Skyla said. "This place is amazing!"

Everything is so different here, Tag thought.

"Look over there!" Blaze said, hopping toward a sparkling blue stream. It was surrounded by tall, pink grass and the water was made up of different blues, like a quilt.

"Perfect," Tag said. "I'm so thirsty." He followed Blaze and Skyla to the stream.

He leaned forward to take a drink when suddenly:

"STOP!" a voice cried.

DANGER!

Tag gripped his dagger while Skyla held up her slingshot.

"Who's there?" Blaze cried.

The three friends looked around, trying to see who had called out to them to stop.

The branches in one of the strange twisted trees began to sway. The pastel-colored cotton-candy balls, which Tag had thought were flowers, suddenly dropped off the tree— one by one. The fluff balls floated down to land at the friends' feet.

Tag looked at the round, fluffy balls. They were creatures with large eyes. They didn't seem to have any arms, legs, feet, or wings.

"SHHH!" the creatures said together.

"Why do we need to be quiet?" Tag whispered.

The creatures stared at the shimmering blue stream with wide eyes. "Don't go near that!" they said.

"Why not?" Skyla asked. "We're really thirsty and—" She froze as the stream began to move.

The strange-looking water began to churn and bubble.

Tag gulped and took a step back. Suddenly, hundreds of large fish with sharp snapping teeth jumped out of the water.

"Snappy fish!" the fluffy creatures yelled. They backed away, their eyes wide and their fur trembling.

The shiny blue fish leaped in and out of the water, snapping their long, spiky teeth at the friends.

One of the fish flew out of the water and landed on the ground near the three friends. It snapped and wriggled toward them slowly, weaving its way through the tall pink grass. Then it grinned at them, showing off its very sharp fangs.

Tag held out his dagger. "Stay back!" he warned the fish. But another fish jumped out of the water, then another, wriggling closer.

Skyla shot an acorn at one of them, but the acorn just bounced off its thick, rubbery skin.

"What should we do?" Skyla asked Tag.

Blaze stepped forward, her feathers bright.

"SKRAAAAAAAA!" she cried.

The snappy fish on land paused, then splashed back into the river, swimming away quickly.

Tag sighed. "We need to be more careful," he told Skyla and Blaze.

Skyla turned to the fluffy creatures. "Thank you," she said. "For warning us."

The fluffy creatures smiled.

"Have you seen any firehawks?" Blaze asked.

The creatures frowned. "No," they said.

"Firehawks look like Blaze," Skyla explained. "They have bright feathers like hers."

"Sorry," they said. "We haven't seen them."

They rolled back to their tree. A gentle breeze filled the air and the creatures floated up one by one back onto the branches.

"I might know where the firehawks are," a small voice said.

One of the fluffy creatures had stayed behind.

"Can you show us?" Tag asked.

The light-pink creature nodded. "Yes, but we must be careful," she said. "In our kingdom, there are things much worse than snappy fish."

THE CLOUDLINGS

The three friends followed after the fluffy creature as she rolled ahead.

"I'm Fifi," she said as she rolled along.

"I'm Tag," Tag replied. "These are my friends, Skyla and Blaze."

"Um . . . I don't mean to be rude," Skyla said. "But what *are* you?"

Fifi giggled. "I'm a cloudling! You've never seen a cloudling before?"

Skyla shook her head. "We're not from around here," she said.

"Thank you for helping us find the firehawks," Blaze added. "So have you really seen birds like me?"

Fifi stopped rolling and looked up at Blaze. "Well . . . the birds I saw were a little bigger than you."

Skyla glanced at Tag nervously. Tag shrugged. "This is the only clue we have," he whispered. "We should keep going."

The sun was still high in the sky, and it seemed to get hotter the farther they walked. Tag wished that the stream hadn't been filled with snappy fish. He was so thirsty!

Fifi started rolling slower and slower.

"Are you okay?" Tag asked. "Should we rest?"

Fifi stopped. "I thought I remembered which way to go, but I don't," she said. "I'm sorry."

"Let's take a break," Skyla said, patting Fifi on the head. "Maybe it will come back to you?"

Tag handed some fruit to Fifi and his friends. He felt a sudden creeping feeling down his feathers and looked up. It was the dark figure again! This time, it was standing a little way ahead beneath a tree.

"Look!" Tag said, pulling out his dagger.

Blaze turned to where Tag was pointing. "I don't see anything," she said.

Skyla frowned. "What did you see?"

Tag walked toward the tree. The shadowy figure had gone. "I thought I saw someone watching us . . ."

Blaze stuck her beak in the sack and pulled out the three golden feathers.

"We need to keep moving, especially if we're being followed," she said. "Maybe the feathers will give me another vision and show us the way."

Something glittered as Blaze moved her wing.

"Whoa!" Tag said.

The feathers had left a sparkle of golden light hanging in the air.

Tag tried to touch the sparkling light. It disappeared.

Blaze waved the feathers back and forth.

"Look!" Skyla gasped. The feathers had left another sparkling trail.

Blaze waved them faster. At first nothing happened, but then their tips began to sparkle. Blaze's eyes shone golden as the feathers made  more marks in the air.

Tag peered closely at the sparkles. "The feathers are making a picture!" he cried.

Fifi's eyes widened. "That looks like the Cloud Kingdom!" she said.

Tag jumped up. "Fifi is right!" he said. "It's a map!"

A MAGICAL MAP

The sparkly map showed all of the Cloud Kingdom. Tag could see the twisty trees where the cloudlings lived. There were also tall mountains, the crystal rocks, and a wide river with a waterfall.

Tag reached out to touch the map. To his surprise, the edges became solid. The sparkly lines turned black, and the map turned into paper.

The paper fluttered to the ground, landing at Tag's feet.

Blaze pointed at an orange dot on the map. "What's that?" she asked.

"I don't know," Tag said.

Skyla, Tag, and Fifi leaned in. The orange dot disappeared for a second then reappeared. It did the same thing again and again.

"The dot is flashing," Skyla said. "The map is trying to show us something."

"Look at those hills," Fifi said, nodding to the map. "Now look up over there."

In the distance, Tag could see three green bumps. "Those are the same hills," he said.

Blaze hopped up and down. "The orange dot must show us where *we* are," she said.

"Yes," Tag agreed.

But then the map began to change. The ink swirled, making strange patterns.

"What's happening to our map?!" Skyla cried.

Tag watched as the ink made a new picture.

A picture of a waterfall sparkled in front of them, but the picture was moving. The water ran along a river and over rocks, crashing into a pool below.

"I think the feathers want us to find that waterfall," Blaze said as the paper went blank.

"Can you take us there?" Tag asked Fifi.

Fifi's fur was shaking. "I'm sorry," she said. "I can't. Cloudlings are afraid of water— even when it's not full of snappy fish."

Skyla hugged Fifi. "I understand," she said. "I am afraid of water, too."

"Thank you for helping us come this far," Tag said.

"You're welcome. Now just head that way, past the hills and into the forest. Good luck!" Fifi rolled away along the path.

Tag studied the blank paper. There was a black smudge on the edge. He blinked. The smudge seemed to be moving. He felt a chill. "The picture has gone, but what's that mark?" he asked.

"What mark?" Skyla asked, leaning in.

Tag pointed to the paper, but the page was entirely blank again. He shook his head and put the map in his sack. "Never mind," he said. "We should keep moving."

They set off, but Tag couldn't help feeling like someone was following them. He thought about what Fifi had said: *In our kingdom, there are things much worse than snappy fish.* What dangers would they find next?

THE WATERFALL

The friends made their way past the hills and into a dark forest. The ground was less bouncy in the woods. There were a few bushes here and there but they were normal colors—greens and browns. Tag felt like he was in Perodia rather than in a strange land.

RRRUMMMBLE!

There was a loud thundering in the distance.

"What's that sound?" Tag asked, holding up his dagger.

The farther they walked, the louder the sound got. Blaze held out her wings, ready to use her fire power.

They soon reached the place where the sound was loudest.

"Let's see what's on the other side of these trees," Skyla said.

Tag took a deep breath and peeked through the trees beside his friends.

He grinned as he saw what was making the sound.

"It's the waterfall!" Skyla laughed.

The noise of the water was deafening as it crashed over huge rocks. The sound echoed through the trees.

"This is not like any waterfall I've ever seen before," Tag said.

The water was not clear or blue. It was every color of the rainbow. Red, orange, yellow, green, blue, purple. The friends stood at the very top of the waterfall. It was a long way down, and the rainbow river that flowed below was wide and fast.

"I feel dizzy!" Skyla said as she looked down. She held on to Blaze's feathers.

"Where are the firehawks?" asked Blaze. "I thought they'd be here . . ."

Tag pulled the paper from his sack, hoping it would hold the answer. But it was still blank. He handed it to Blaze.

As soon as Blaze touched it, swirls of ink appeared on the paper again. It showed the waterfall. Three small figures were standing beside it now.

"That's us!" Skyla said, pointing to the three figures.

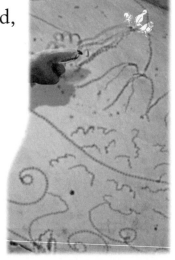

The three figures moved across the paper toward the waterfall.

"We have to cross the waterfall," Blaze said.

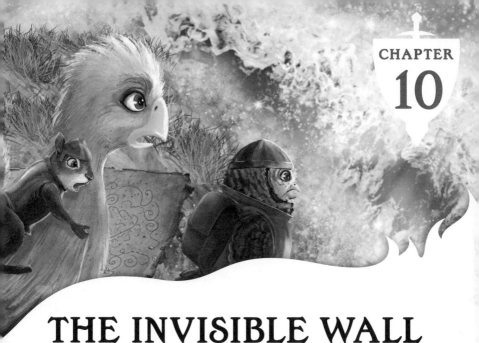

THE INVISIBLE WALL

The friends stared at the rushing water.

"How can we cross the waterfall?" Tag asked. "There's no bridge."

"We will have to fly over it," Blaze said.

Tag noticed the dark smudge on the edge of the paper again. "What if there's something bad waiting for us on the other side?"

"What if my family is over there?" Blaze replied. She gave the paper to Tag, and he tucked it back in his sack. Blaze opened her wings.

She took off, so Tag followed. "We'll be right back!" Tag called out to Skyla, who watched from the edge of the water.

But as soon as Blaze and Tag got close to the waterfall, a great wind and spray of water pushed them back. They tried again but it felt like there was an invisible wall holding them back.

"It's no good," Tag said, landing back where they'd begun. "We'll have to find another way."

"Skyla?" Blaze called out. Skyla was nowhere to be seen.

"Over here!" she replied, poking her head out of some bushes a little farther down. "I found a secret path behind the waterfall. We should follow it."

"Are you sure you can do this?" Tag asked. He knew Skyla was terrified of water.

Skyla nodded. "It may be the only way across."

Tag and Blaze followed her through the bushes and onto a narrow ledge behind the waterfall. They carefully shuffled along, staying close to the rock wall.

Whooooooooooo! A whistling sound filled the air.

The wind blew harder and harder. *It's strange for the wind to be so strong back here, Tag thought. It's as if someone—or something— doesn't want us to reach the other side.* He held on to Blaze and Skyla so that they weren't swept over the waterfall.

The water fell faster and heavier beside them. The roar of the water filled the air.

"Watch out!" Blaze shouted.

Just then, the strange and powerful wind swept the wall of water into one gigantic wave. It surged toward them.

"Get beneath my wings!" Blaze yelled.

She pulled Tag and Skyla close, then wrapped her strong wings around them all, tucking her head inside.

Tag could hear the water pounding on Blaze's wings. *I hope we don't get swept over the edge!* he thought.

When Blaze was sure that the wave had passed, she opened her wings. "Are you okay?" she asked.

"Yes, thank you!" said Skyla.

"Now let's get out of here," Tag said. "We're almost through to the other side."

Suddenly, a blur of orange and red and gold burst through the water! Sharp talons swooped down and grabbed Blaze.

"Blaze!" Tag and Skyla shouted. But before they could move—

Blaze was gone.

THE PEAHOG

"**B**laze!" Skyla shouted at the wall of water.
Skyla and Tag were all alone on the ledge.

"What happened?" Skyla cried, her fur
trembling.

"I don't know," Tag said. "But we need to
find Blaze. Come on!"

He shuffled along the ledge as fast as he could. Skyla held on to his wing.

Finally, they came out the other side of the waterfall. There were no trees or bushes on this side. Just a wide open valley with two snow-covered mountains in the distance.

"Where is she?" Skyla said. "Do you think she's okay?"

"I'll try to find her from above," Tag said. He took off into the sky, searching for any sign of Blaze or of the creature that had snatched her away.

"Can you see anything?" Skyla called from below.

Tag scanned the sky. Ahead were the mountains. Below there was nothing but—

Something moved among the grass!

Tag swooped down, and landed in the grass. Skyla raced over and stood beside him, holding out her slingshot.

A small, colorful creature stood before them. The creature had a round snout like a pig, and a curly tail. Its body was covered in blue and green and purple feathers. Its green eyes were wide with fear.

"Where is Blaze?" Tag asked the creature.

"What's a blaze?" the creature asked.

Tag put away his dagger and sighed. "I'm Tag and this is Skyla."

The creature smiled. "I'm Zeb," he said. "I'm a peahog."

"It's nice to meet you," Skyla added.

"Blaze is our friend," Tag explained. "We were all behind the waterfall. Then a creature with orange and red feathers grabbed Blaze and carried her away."

"The creature had very long, sharp claws," Skyla added. "Have you seen anything like that?"

Zeb nodded. "I've seen birds like that," he said. "They live over there."

He pointed at the mountains.

"Thank you, Zeb!" Tag said.

"There is a valley that runs between those two mountains," Zeb said. "It's the quickest way to the birds' nests. Follow the path and it will lead you there. But don't leave the path."

"Why?" Skyla asked.

Zeb frowned. "You don't want to find out."

Tag shivered, thinking about Zeb's warning: *Don't leave the path.*

Then Zeb wandered off through the grass. "Good luck!" he called.

FOLLOW THE PATH

Tag and Skyla walked toward the mountains ahead of them.

"It might be quicker if we fly," Tag said. "We can follow the path from the sky."

Skyla put her hand on her hip. "I can't fly without Blaze."

"Ah," said Tag. "Good point. We'll have to walk."

"Besides," Skyla added. "Zeb said to stay *on* the path."

Tag and Skyla walked on through a valley covered in tall pink grass.

"I really hope Blaze is okay," Skyla said.

"She has her firehawk powers to protect her," Tag said. "But we need to find her soon."

Skyla nodded.

Tag tried to keep to the path like Zeb had told them, but the grass grew tall and wild.

Tag stopped walking. "I can't see the path anymore," he said. "The grass grew over it."

Skyla whistled. "It doesn't look like anyone has been this way for a very long time," she said.

"I'll fly ahead quickly, just to see if I can find the path again," Tag said.

"Okay, but hurry back!" Skyla called after her friend.

Tag flew ahead. Farther along, he saw a dark line in the grass.

He flew down closer. There was another wiggly brown line. And another. The squiggly lines were moving through the tall grass. And they were heading toward Skyla!

I should never have left the path! Tag's heart raced as he flew back to Skyla as fast as he could. But he was too late.

"Giant snakes!" Tag shouted.

Giant snakes surrounded Skyla. They slithered around her in a circle, moving closer and closer.

"**HISSSSSSSSSS!**" A huge snake reared its head and hissed at Skyla.

"Help!" Skyla screamed.

Tag swooped over her head. "Quick! Grab my tail feathers," he called.

Skyla held on tight, and Tag flapped as hard as he could. Slowly, Skyla lifted off the ground. Tag tried to fly away from the snakes, but Skyla was heavy.

Tag's feathers shook. The snakes were big enough to gobble them up whole.

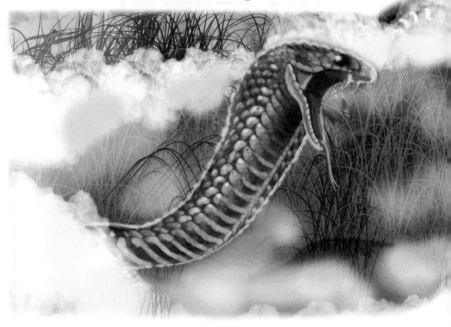

"Tasssssty sssssnack!" one snake hissed.

"Eeeeek!" Skyla yelled as another snake showed its fangs.

Tag took a deep breath and flapped harder. He didn't stop flapping until they were through the valley, with the snakes far behind.

"Phew!" Skyla said. "You really saved my tail there."

Tag puffed. "We need to get out of here in case they follow us," he said. "Let's find those birds' nests!"

They hurried out of the valley and up a steep hill.

Skyla gasped when they reached the top. Far in the distance, she could see a group of large, colorful birds. Their feathers glowed gold and orange and red in the sunlight as they landed in the valley below.

"Are those—" Tag started to say.

"Firehawks!" Skyla cried. "We've finally found them!"

FIREHAWKS!

Skyla ran down the hill toward the birds.

"Wait!" Tag called after her.

He squinted at the birds, trying to get a better look. They had the same colorful feathers as Blaze, but something didn't seem quite right.

Suddenly, the birds all took to the sky as one. They flew off toward some tall trees far, far in the distance. Then they were gone.

"I'm not sure those birds are firehawks," Tag said, landing beside Skyla.

"But they have to be!" Skyla cried. She raced farther down the hill.

Tag flew after her and landed in a small clearing close to where they had seen the birds. "Do you see any sign of Blaze?"

But Skyla was staring at the ground, trembling. "Tag," she said in a shaky voice. "I think you were right . . ."

Tag looked down. They were standing inside a *gigantic* bird footprint.

"A firehawk didn't leave that," Tag said.

"Tag, what if those giant birds thought Blaze was their dinner?" Skyla said. "Or what if they've taken her far away? She could be in real danger!"

"Blaze is strong," Tag reminded his friend. "And we *will* find her."

Skyla looked at Tag's sack, then gasped.

"The feathers!" she said. "We still have the feathers and the paper and the Ember Stone. Maybe *they* can help us find Blaze?"

"Let's try!" Tag said.

Skyla quickly unrolled the paper. Tag placed the Ember Stone on it like they had done with Grey's magical map. Skyla held the three golden feathers and waved them back and forth like Blaze had done.

"Where is Blaze?" she said out loud.

Tag watched the map. But it stayed blank.

"Nothing is happening!" Skyla cried.

"Wait!" Tag said. "Look!"

The tips of the golden feathers had started to glow.

Skyla held them over the paper. "Where is Blaze?" she asked again, louder this time.

The feathers jumped out of Skyla's paw and started to draw on the paper.

TO THE RESCUE

The feathers scribbled faster and faster until they dropped to the ground.

Skyla and Tag peered at the paper. The feathers had drawn a picture.

"I see the tall trees," Tag said, "and some nests."

"Blaze!" Skyla cried as the picture changed to show Blaze sitting inside a nest. "Those giant birds *did* take her!"

Then the sparkling lines swirled and changed into a new picture. This one showed Tag and Skyla on one side. On the other side was a patch of tall trees.

"I think the feather is telling us that we need to head to those trees. Just like when it showed us we needed to go to the waterfall," Skyla said.

As Skyla hurried to pack away their supplies, Tag glanced at the paper again. The black smudge was back! It was close to where he and Skyla stood. A cold shiver went through his feathers as he thought about the dark figure he had seen on Fire Island and again in the Cloud Kingdom. It made him feel just like he had felt whenever Thorn and The Shadow were close.

"Skyla," Tag said. "I know Thorn and The Shadow are gone. But what if there is something far worse here in the Cloud Kingdom?"

Skyla didn't answer. Instead, she held Tag's wing.

Tag swallowed down his fear. "The birds flew in this direction," he said, pointing ahead.

Tag pulled out his dagger, and Skyla held her slingshot. "Let's go," she said. "It's time to get our friend back!"

ABOUT THE AUTHOR

KATRINA CHARMAN has wanted to be a children's book writer ever since she was eleven, when her teacher asked her class to write an epilogue to Roald Dahl's *Matilda*. Katrina's teacher thought her writing was good enough to send to Roald Dahl himself! Sadly, she never got a reply, but this experience ignited her love of reading and writing. Katrina lives in England with her husband and three daughters. The Last Firehawk is her first early chapter book series in the U.S.

ABOUT THE ILLUSTRATOR

JUDIT TONDORA was born in Hungary. She is an illustrator and graphic designer who has worked for various clients in the world of publishing and commercial design. Today, she enjoys working from her countryside studio where she can see animals just like Tag and Skyla out her window!

Questions and Activities

1. **W**hat is a portal? (Hint! Reread page 7.) What does the portal to Cloud Kingdom look like? How do the friends open it?

2. **I**n book one, Tag, Skyla, and Blaze visit Fire Island. What did it look like then? What is different about the island now?

 3. **T**ag thinks someone—or something—is watching him. Find two examples.

4. **W**hat happens to Blaze when the friends cross the waterfall? What do you think will happen next, and why?

5. **T**he friends discover new creatures, plants, and sights in Cloud Kingdom. Draw and label your own addition to the kingdom!